The January Estate

Charles Wilkinson

The January Estate
by Charles Wilkinson
ISBN: 978-1-908125-99-6

Cover Art by David Rix

Publication Date: 2022

For Derek and Verena Cannon

Contents

Winter Both Ways

Alick Strang lay flat on the top of his desk. For the last ten minutes, he'd been imagining himself as immune to sensation: a medieval effigy, with closed, marmoreal eyelids, stone-still on top of his tomb. Yet he remained aware of the relics of the previous night's drinking: the gastric burn, a pulsing nausea, the iron band on his forehead, the visor of cold sweat. By way of distraction, he turned his head towards the plate-glass windows and gazed out. Above the tree line, soft grey curls of whitish cloud moved just beneath a fathomless grey sky.

The wall clock told him he would be immured in the room for another fifty minutes. He tried to picture himself inside a tomb: a hollow stomach, nothing to feel queasy with; the head no longer pounding and leaden, but empty, the dry air inside it motionless; the skull a bony world beyond perception. What about the Metaphysical poets? No, it would be quite wrong to have them soiled by inevitable incomprehension.

A faint, continuous scratching: cobwebs of sound woven from several quarters of the room. Bad – in that he was reminded of *their* presence; good – in that *they* were still writing, absorbed by the task he'd set them and therefore unlikely to disturb him for a while yet. But would it keep them occupied for the entire double period? He had nothing else prepared. The thought of having to bluff his way through the final quarter of an hour induced a tremor of panic to compete with his dry tongue and aching forehead.

The previous day he'd floundered from lesson to lesson before sinking at 6.00 into a warm bath of alcohol. During morning prayers, he'd come up with a strategy to see himself through the day. His first two lessons were with the scholarship class. There was a set of papers he'd intended to use later in the week. An obvious solution.

The sound of the door opening. Why couldn't people knock?

"Mr Strang!"

The Headmaster's voice, surprised; Strang swung himself off the table. Placing one arm on the swivel chair for support proved a mistake: as it moved, he lurched giddily.

"Er … sorry. My bad back – it plays up in the mornings."

"A word, if you please. In the corridor would be best. I see work has been set. Please continue, boys."

Alick shuffled out, stooping slightly.

"At least they're quiet, but I'm not entirely convinced, Strang. Especially as you only joined us in January, with the academic year well under way. A more energetic approach is needed, especially before break! Otherwise they'll soon see through you."

The Headmaster was a lithe athletic man in late middle age, his wings of grey hair brushed back over his ears. He wore a cricket jumper under a well-cut blue blazer, trainers and sharply pressed cavalry twill trousers. Had he been supervising indoor cricket nets? His expression implied he'd narrowly restrained himself from raising his finger; one more infringement and it would be the long walk back to the pavilion.

"I'm sorry. It won't happen again."

"Now about the other matter. The key to the cupboard in your classroom. I've asked the Bursar and he can't locate it. Your predecessor, David Midstair, would obviously have had one, but he left us hurriedly at the end of December. No doubt he forgot to return his key to the Bursar's Office. The whereabouts of the spare one are a mystery."

"I would like to get in there soon. If it's convenient …"

"It will be impossible for the maintenance staff to open your cupboard immediately. That is not say you shouldn't put in a request to Mr Amble and his men. No doubt one of them will find a solution in the fullness of time."

"It's about checking the available stock … being able to access past papers."

"There are adequate resources on the open shelves," he said, glancing at his watch. "You'd best get back to your class. I fancy I hear a low whispering."

"We've finished," put in a boy in the front row, almost before Alick had stepped back into the classroom.

"Well, check your work."

"I've checked mine!"

"Check it again."

Strang sank back into the swivel chair and picked up the scholarship paper, which was set by a school he'd never heard of. A poem by a writer with an unfamiliar name and ten questions underneath. Neglecting to read through it before sending it to the secretary for photocopying had been a mistake. He scanned the opening three stanzas: completely incomprehensible. After rubbing his eyes and taking a deep breath, he went through the poem three times. It became more baffling with successive readings. The title had no bearing on the rest of the text, as far as he could see. The questions? Every one of them was unanswerable.

The atmosphere in the Common Room had a strong suggestion of aeroplanes shot down in flames; a whiff of a burnt fuselage in the tobacco smoke. The Squadron Leader's expression was fixed at smooth flat angles, the result of painstaking facial reconstruction at the hands of a fine surgeon; his twisted, scar-white hand gripped a pencil hovering over a cryptic crossword.

Break had begun five minutes ago. Cups of acrid coffee were being carried to battered leather armchairs. There was nowhere for Strang to sit. The lady covering the Reception Class had draped the last available seat with unfinished knitting. He pretended to read the notice board.

"So you're the new geographer?"

The voice came from somewhere below him. Strang glanced down. The Wing Commander stared up at him from the depths of a sagging, dung-coloured sofa.

"No, English."

"I thought you were the replacement for … the fellow who thought he could teach geography. The name will come to me in a minute." The Wing Commander bit on the stem of his pipe and sucked vigorously.

"I've taken over from David Midstair."

The Wing Commander glared at Strang, as if fixing a Messerschmitt in his cross hairs.

"Midstair? I knew that a new geography man was coming after Christmas. That was certainly no surprise after what happened to 4C. But Midstair!" He turned towards the Squadron Leader. "Did you hear that? Midstair has been given the order of the boot."

"What's that, Winco?" The voice was grating; an engine in need of oil.

"Midstair … a goner. Sacked!"

"I don't think so. Last I heard he'd been sent upstairs. On night duties from now on."

"If he is still coming in," said Strang. "I'd very much like to speak to him. I haven't been able to unlock the cupboard …"

"He won't have a word to say to you," put in the Squadron Leader. "Not while you've still got a desk job."

"Don't try to get into that cupboard without the support of ground staff," added the Wing Commander. "Midstair would have a key though, wouldn't he, Squadron Leader?"

"Two … at the very least."

The tobacco smoke thickened, obscuring the lady knitting on the sofa. Now only the steady click of needles implied her continuing presence. Strang coughed uncontrollably; best to get out while he could see an exit through the fug.

Outside, the younger boys wheeled, flying and re-forming in ever varying groups; some of the older ones sat on benches or played games of football on the paddock next to the winter-grey playing-ground, a mixture of thin grass and sandy topsoil. He recognized the eight boys in the scholarship class playing an unseasonal game of croquet. There was a marked physical similarity between them: mouse-coloured hair and thin pallid faces, a slight build that suggested a former athleticism; their movements graceful yet slow, somehow convalescent.

A polyphony of high voices – shouting screaming, babbling, laughing – mingled with the creak of the swings, the background thrum of the busy road beyond the fir trees and dense, dark rhododendrons. In the midst of the movement, the duty master could be seen, standing in scarf and duffle coat, a mug gripped in mitted hands, a plume of white breath rising into the January air. As Strang made his way through the throng of boys, he recognized him: Simon Hance, senior French and middle-school R.E.

"Break duty. The worst time of the week," said the master. "Still, at least there have been no deaths so far. How are you getting on?"

"Fine, I hope. The main problem is there's apparently no way of getting into the cupboard in my form room."

"Your predecessor always kept it locked. It was part of the Midstair mystique – having a cupboard no one else could get into."

"Really? I've been assuming that there's departmental stock in there: poetry anthologies, form readers, examination papers – that sort of thing."

"No one can say those things aren't in there. But rumour has it Midstair used the place as some kind of private oratory."

"I'd like to check it out. The Wing Commander says that Midstair must have a spare key."

"You haven't been in the Old Common Room, have you? Everyone teaching here full-time has to use the Staff Room. Didn't the Head tell you that?"

"No."

"I wouldn't go in there without your wings, if I were you. I'm not saying they're a bad lot. All of them taught here, most with some distinction. But if you're not careful they'll start to want to cover for you. Take the odd lesson here and there – or do lunch duty. That sort of thing. The next thing you know is your pay packet will be docked."

The bell rang. Somewhere in the distance came the sound of a siren, the faint suggestion of pilots about to scramble; a whiff of petrol and oily rags on the breeze. Boys headed towards the entrance with differing degrees of reluctance. The wind blew feathers of soft sand over the playground.

He arrived five minutes late for a class to find the Wing Commander in charge, the boys sitting silently, a pile of exercise books stacked neatly in the middle of the table.

"Ah, you're here!" said the Winco. He was standing by a window and puffing on a briar pipe. "I don't mind staying a little longer if you're busy, old boy."

"No, that's quite all right. I'll take over, thanks," said Strang, sweeping a set of short story anthologies off the shelves.

"They're as keen as mustard, this lot. Couldn't prevent them from handing in their books even though I suggested they wait for you. Are you sure you wouldn't like someone to cover your back for bit? A tail-end, Charlie."

"I can manage now."

"Oh well, probably just as well. The Head doesn't like me smoking in the classroom."

As soon as the Winco was through the door, Strang told a pupil in the back row to shut the window.

"When will we have our results, sir?' the boy said, even before standing up.

The entire school was at congregational practice. Sensing it a good time to try to track down the maintenance staff, Strang slipped out after the first hymn. Everyone he'd spoken to agreed that Mr. Amble and his men existed but no one could tell him where to find them. He was told they were 'round and about in the grounds', 'decorating one of the dormitories', 'marking out a pitch on the other side of the copse', 'servicing the second largest lawn mower', 'replacing a broken tile on the Head's house'. But when he went to these places there was no sign of them. There were rumours of a shed where they convened to drink stupendous mugs of strong tea, avoid instructions and swap tales about the boiler room. Once he'd caught a glimpse of a bent figure with a wheelbarrow moving through the entrance to the walled garden.

On his way to breakfast, Strang saw slow-moving, grizzled shapes shifting indefinable burdens through the mist. At dusk, there was faint red light in one of the windows of an outhouse by the staff car park, but when he moved closer it went out. Perhaps it was only a reflection, the rear end of a vehicle moving away, or a gleam from the last of the sunlit west.

The extent of the school site was larger than Strang had realized. The original Tudor mansion had been restored by the Victorians before being encased in a white modernist shell with a flat roof. The architect had also designed a series of classrooms, laboratories and assembly halls that resembled aircraft hangars, as well as a staff accommodation block in the shape of a control tower. Inside the main building, the rooms were smaller than expected, as if they were boxes inside a series of much larger boxes. Yet the campus seemed designed for several thousand pupils and not the hundred and ninety-three on the roll.

How was he going to discover where the maintenance staff was based except by chance? Then he remembered: he'd not yet tried the Bursar's Office, which was in the main building. He'd been certain where it was, but after several wrong turnings he found himself walking down a red-tiled corridor beyond the Old Common Room. Right at the very end was a black oak door with a wooden lintel. An enormous iron key was in the lock. Strang turned it and went in: darkness and dust, yet also the scent of chalk and sawdust, and something sharper, a fixative perhaps; yes, the heady aroma of glue. It was a moment before he found a light switch. A classroom, long since disused; shutters over the windows; a free-standing blackboard in the corner, textbooks crumbling on the shelves; wooden desks, their lids scored, furrowed, gouged, potholed by pairs of compasses, initialled with penknives; some desks mapped with dark blue – the accidental cartography of spilt ink. Then he saw them: the model aeroplanes suspended from the ceiling. Spitfires, Hurricanes, Lancasters, but Junkers and Heinkels too; at the end of its thread, a Dornier circled very slowly in a draught. On the lockers at the back of the room were kits in various stages of assembly, along with a flight of balsa wood planes powered by rubber bands, some with no propellers or skeletal fuselages. Behind the silence ... the whisper of war, the dead boys' distant crying of Latin tags: *cave; ad astra ....*

At senior lunch, Strang found himself at the head of a table with three 8A pupils; one of them, a long-faced boy with almond-shaped green eyes about to vanish into his grey skin, was on his left, serving vegetables. He said: "We've got you next, sir; haven't we?"

"Yes."

"Will you be going through our papers?"

"No, I thought we might do the form reader this afternoon."

"Again!"

"We'll go through the paper in due course."

"How did I get on, sir?"

"Umm ... I'll let you know soon."

Towards the end of the meal, the boy turned to one of his classmates and said *sotte voce*: "He hasn't even marked them yet."

His friend leant over and murmured: "Does anyone know the point of Mr. Strang?"

After grace, Alick left quickly for the refuge of the staff room. For once, he was first to the coffee machine and so able to help Simon Hance, who'd been outside supervising junior break, to a cup.

"Thanks," said his colleague. "I need this. I've got the scholars next. They're very quick. Wide awake, even after lunch."

"I thought I had them for English."

"Surely … oh … I see! You haven't realised there are two scholarship groups. Everyone in your set is down for the same destination; they can be taught as a group. 8S are all bound for different schools, which makes life very difficult. Still, I have heard your lot are rather rarefied, head-in-the-air types. So perhaps it's as well I don't take them."

In contrast to conditions in the Old Common Room, the younger staff enjoyed a bright space with high windows and an atrium overhead. It was part of a recent extension built in a *faux* eighteenth-century manner with walls brightly painted in Regency yellow. The quality of light was different to the pervasive gloom of the Tudor and Victorian interiors, but not unlike the hangar-like outbuildings, where a strange disturbance had seeped into the space, suffusing the atmosphere with the imminence of departure.

"To be honest, I'm not keen on them either. They're kicking up because I haven't gone through their wretched scholarship paper."

"Well, why don't you do that?"

As soon as they were sitting down on a sofa well away from the rest of the staff, Strang leaned forward. "Keep this to yourself. It's hard to admit to a total lack of competence, but I've never come across such a paper before. It's utterly incomprehensible. I can't understand a single line of the poem. If only I can find the answer sheet then ..."

"Why seek yesterday's solutions to today's questions?"

"I'm sorry?"

"It sounds as if this text of yours may be resistant to a definitive interpretation. Why should there be right and wrong answers to the questions? And even if there were, wouldn't they vary according to the spatial and temporal circumstances of the readers. The moment in history when they're asked to respond to the text."

"But surely there must be some kernel of agreement ... not just this ... epidemic of uncertainty."

"Have you looked to see what the boys have come up with?"

"Yes, they've all written at considerable length, but at no point are their explanations even slightly similar."

"Exactly. Each response is a fresh encounter with a text yielding multiple readings." Hance picked up his leather bag and rose. "Here's what I'd do. Assume everyone's answers are a hundred per cent correct; then deduct marks for spelling and punctuation mistakes as well as inadequate presentation. That way you'll be able to return their books without giving them identical marks."

As Strang made his way back down the corridor towards his classroom, the bell for lessons rang. Somewhere within that sound was an echo of a siren, a suggestion of distant figures scrambling for shelters or men running quickly across the tarmac a few moments before the engines began to turn.

On Monday morning, Strang overslept and discovered himself fifteen minutes late for the first period, which was with 8A. As he hurried towards his classroom, he saw the door was ajar. He could hear boys speaking, not conversationally but clearly, one at a time. Was an adult, the Headmaster perhaps, in there with them? Excuses ran through his mind: a violent attack of vomiting from which he'd only just recovered; a phone call informing him of the death of his brother; his alarm clock malfunctioning after a mysterious power cut, apparently restricted to his room.

The Wing Commander was standing behind the desk, holding an examination paper in his right hand; a pipe smoldered in his left, the scent of tobacco redolent of a more manly age. There was a profound solidity to his thick tweed suit, its check neither too bold nor blandly patterned, and his striped tie, with its reliable Windsor knot. A monocle dangled from a cord. The exercise books had been handed out and the boys were either looking at them attentively or had their eyes fixed on the Wing Commander, who was answering a question with evident authority.

"Good morning, dear boy," he said, turning in mid-sentence towards Strang. "I hope you don't mind my climbing into your cockpit! Only I happened to be passing and found these fine young fellows unsupervised."

"The Winco … I mean 'sir' … is going through our paper," said a boy in the front row.

Was he the one Strang had sat next to at lunch? Today they looked more alike than ever, uniformly pale yet resolute, as if ready for combat.

"I don't mind going on with this lesson, since I've started."

"Please let the Winco finish, sir. He's a jolly good teacher," put in someone at the back. There was a general murmur of agreement.

"Oh …" said Strang. "In that case, if you don't mind, Wing Commander …"

"Not at all, dear boy. Absolutely delighted!"

Strang made his way back to the Staff Room. He had a double free next and some middle school marking to catch up on. Would it be too much to expect the Wing Commander to correct 8A's books?

The Headmaster sent for him after lunch. Part of his study was in the old building, but there was a modern extension with a photocopier and a desk for a secretary. In one corner behind his desk were cricket bats, a hockey stick, several tennis racquets and a croquet mallet.

"I hear you were late on parade this morning, Strang. And what's worse is the Wing Commander stepped in and took your lesson. Am I right?"

"Yes, I wasn't at my best. A slight …"

"Well, if you're sick, man … ring in! We'll find someone from the Staff Room to cover for you. Now the school's paying twice for that lesson. You're salaried and the Wing Commander will put in his fee. You can be sure of that."

"I'm sorry, but it might not have been a bad thing for them to have a change from me. To be frank, I haven't been having a lot of joy with them. The last time they seemed completely lifeless and …"

"Now listen here," said the Headmaster, standing up. He was wearing a blue tracksuit and a metal whistle on a lanyard. "It's not a simple matter of the quick and the dead, but a question of two conditions of time existing simultaneously. As you can imagine, this creates all kinds of administrative problems."

"I'm hoping to make a fresh start with them."

"You'll be lucky. I'm still looking into it but I'm told the Wing Commander has taken 8A off to the Old History Room. It'll be a job to get them out of there."

"I think I know where that is … I'll …"

"*Nothing* is what you'll do. This is going to mean complicated negotiations with traffic control. I'm afraid you're going to have to teach some geography … 4C. It's not their favourite subject. I'll be looking to you to enthuse them."

After last lesson, he met Simon Hance, who was doing some photocopying in the Staff Room. "You know there's something quite soothing about using this machine on the rare occasions when it's working properly. The sheets sliding through as if there was no such thing as a paper jam … I hear you've lost 8 Aeronautical for English."

"Yes, I'm going to teach some geography instead."

"Everyone who's earthbound ends up teaching geography eventually."

"I've got 4C."

"Oh dear."

"They're not that keen on the subject, I'm told."

"Their previous teacher was unsuited to the profession. Even so, there was no excuse for what he did."

"And what was that? When I ask people, they clam up."

"We're not supposed to speak about it. But if you're going to teach that form you ought to know. He blew his brains out in front of them. Five minutes before the end of a lesson on glaciation, which isn't even on the Middle School syllabus. Things hadn't been going at all well, apparently."

Strang woke up early. He'd dreamt of terminal moraines in the shape of graves. Unable to sleep, he decided to go to his classroom and make a start on marking 4C's exercise books. For once there was sharp sunlight instead of morning mist. Inside, the light filtering through the blinds hovered halfway between watery milk and velvet, blurring the edges of hard objects. It took Strang a moment to realise the door to the cupboard was wide open. Nearest to him was a shelf filled, not with text books or examination papers, but confiscated objects: marbles and golf balls, penknives, jacks, a wooden ruler sharpened to a point; a dart, a catapult; tennis balls, white in colour, almost bald, or a yellow close to green; a comic, its title long discontinued. A faint musty smell; moments captured by the past, never to be returned. There was a whole school photograph in a broken frame. David Midstair was sitting right at the end of the staff row. A quirk of the light made him appear more insubstantial than his colleagues, his pale face and white hair on the point of evaporation.

As Strang moved further into the cupboard, his eyes slowly adjusted to the dark. Right at the back, where he'd expected to find a wall, there was a staircase. He turned round. Behind him, his classroom seemed a long way off, as if the laws of perspective had suffered a strange adjustment, or he was seeing the present through the lens of the past. Once he started to climb upwards, he heard footsteps above him. At first, he thought it could only be one person, but as he closed the gap, he realised there were several steadily rising ahead of him. There was no light. He was reliant on a handrail and the sounds above, which were of a purposeful, unhurried ascent with no trace of panic. Was he moving towards a kind of conclusion, one he would be a part of – or would the stairs snake upwards forever?

The movements above him faded into silence. Then he saw a square of grey sky. A vertical ladder … a few rungs. At last he was standing on the long flat roof at the summit of the school building.

On the horizon, streaks of silvery dawn and subdued pink, casting sufficient light to suggest the landscape below had changed. To his left, a main road had vanished; the surrounding fields were smaller. Even the width of the river was swollen after a long-forgotten flood. Shadows suggested the contours of an earlier map showing through; something hidden but preserved, now visible, an impossibility at hand.

When he turned to the right, he saw half a dozen small figures walking with a group of men towards the Spitfires. One at the back, who was holding a helmet, turned round. In the slanting light, Strang recognized the face of a boy who'd sat in the front row of 8A. Then he saw the white face of the Squadron Leader; next to him the Wing Commander, leaning towards a boy, no doubt murmuring words of encouragement. The third figure was practically transparent, his head on the verge of vanishing in a halo of mist. Was this David Midstair?

The first pilot climbed into the cockpit. The top of the building was tarmac now, a runway extending far beyond the bounds of the roof. Another place had permeated the school and its surroundings. Strang was on an aerodrome, the countryside around it flat. A cold breeze from the coast; scents of fuel and salt on the air. The sunlight brightened, glinting on a propeller as it began to rotate; the aircrew fled to the periphery. The first Spitfire taxied, turned, collecting speed and glamour, and lifted up towards the gathering dawn. A second then followed it, and a third. The first Spitfire to fly was still just visible, a neat incision on the slow escalation of blue, when the last plane rose into the air, carrying the whole scene away with it, like a vast sheet of paper snapping and rolling with the wind.

Strang was alone on the roof, the sky still slick and shining for a moment; the brilliance of the past dried on the screen of the present. He knew he had to go at once down through the building, away from this parallel January, out of the door and into his classroom, where another winter awaited him.

Double-Sided Haunts

I

Thomas Wall's first recollection of the house was of looking straight through the open door to the blue sea on the far side. At six he'd made his first visit there during the dying days of summer. He turned seven in September and would soon be sent to boarding school. His parents weren't invited inside and so he was left with the impression that the estate consisted of a facade and extensive gardens. At that age it was allowable for him to mistake the janitor, who walked with them as far as the wellingtonia and the horse chestnuts, for the man who owned the property.

During his first term away from home he dreamt of the house, often as if it were part of a film set, but sometimes more vividly: to pass through the threshold was a form of diving into the limitless expanse of the ocean; the experience not one of drowning but of being assimilated by water. Thomas tried to explain this to a close friend but lacked the words to provide more than a partial explanation.

When he was at home, he dreamt less often of the house: the portico first seen from the gravel path as he approached, the letting go of his parents' hands as he walked up the stone steps to the threshold, the blue immensity bounded by no more than a distant border of sky, pale at the point where it met the sea. Once he dreamt of the janitor, a tall man with a high forehead and a beard.

The week before he was due to return to school, he asked his father about the house: "When are we going to go back to that … place?"

"Which place?"

"You remember! The long grey building with an open door and a garden."

"We won't need to go there for several years."

"Are we related to the owner? The man who talked about the trees?"

"No, he was looking after the house while the owner was away."

"When we next visit, will the owner be there?"

"I don't think so. At least we won't see him," said his father, picking up his newspaper and spreading it on the kitchen table.

"But Daddy! What's the point of having a house if you never go in it?"

His father turned several pages before answering. Without looking at Thomas, he replied: "Some say he is always absent; others claim that if you search hard enough, you'll find he was there the whole time."

When Thomas looked back on it, it was strange how clearly he recalled the events of those days. The two brothers arrived in the middle of his third term at boarding school. Hugh Brooks, the younger by a year, had pale, refined features. He appeared perpetually half asleep, even at times on the edge of fading into another, more languorous world. Thane had a darker complexion and black hair that curled over his collar, a style normally deemed impermissible at the school. He was altogether more alert and argumentative.

That summer, Thane was in Thomas's dormitory. An instigator of petty feuds and pedlar of ill-advised adventures, he was a fractious presence from the start. Ever ready to taunt those who declined his dares, he was disliked by most but nonetheless quickly established himself as someone it was imprudent to cross. Even the prefect supposedly in charge was wary of him.

Thomas awoke at around ten o'clock to find Thane seated on the side of his bed. On the longest day of the year, the dormitory was suffused with a soft silvery radiance even though it was late.

Thomas turned over and looked at Thane, a face shimmering above him in the velvet light that seemed also an insufficient darkness.

"Hello, Wall," he said gently. "I'm going to take you apart, brick by brick."

"Go away, Brooks. I want to sleep."

"Well, it's the next best thing to death, isn't it," he said, getting up. In spite of the lingering warmth, he wore a long dark dressing-gown, its silk sleek as night.

"What? Are you trying to give me nightmares?"

"Good night, Wall. Remember it's an empty skull that has no dreams."

A few weeks before the end of term, just after the examinations, demob devilry was in the air. The prefect had begun to speak of leavers' pranks; a perfect time for transgressions. In the dormitory, it was Thane who suggested an evening diversion, a test of nerve. Late June heat was heavy in the air, even though the high sash windows in most of the dormitories were open at the bottom. Outside, a ledge ran along the brickwork. Brooks claimed he could walk across it and climb through the window of the adjoining dormitory. No, that would be impossible, someone objected; you couldn't just dance along the ledge as if it were a tightrope. Agreed, Brooks replied, but the windows were close together and the brickwork was worn; there were plenty of handholds.

The next night he proved it. Several boys leant out of the window to watch his progress, which they later said was surprisingly swift, as if he'd taken the route many times before. Thomas and one other boy stayed in their beds. Even if the lookouts had not kept up a continuous commentary, Thomas would have known that Brooks had arrived safely from the applause next door.

"Your turn soon, Wall," said Brooks, the next day.

"You can't make me."

"Oh, but I think everyone in our dorm will want to see you try. Wall's walk. By popular demand!"

Thomas didn't go next. That night in the dormitory, Matron made them kneel beside their beds and say their prayers. She mumbled goodnight, the gin already silting her Irish tongue. Half an hour later, Thane Brooks sprang out of bed, sat on top of the chest of drawers and addressed the dorm. Everyone was awake. Fear thickened in the humid summer night.

"I've shown you how it's done. So who's up for it tonight? Personally, I've preference for … Wall. A very solid type."

"What about Burnett? He's been the most annoying," said the prefect. A pale thin boy with almost albino-white hair and damp blue eyes,

Burnett was as quick to boast as to blub, over-talkative and ever ready to ingratiate himself with authority. Like Thomas, he'd stayed in bed the previous night.

"Fine," said Thane. "Let's vote. Those for Wall, hands up! Any abstentions? No. Right, those for Burnett … by two votes Burnett's our boy tonight. Sorry Wall, you'll have to wait till tomorrow."

"But I don't want to," wailed Burnett. "It wasn't a fair vote. And you said Wall should go first, didn't you, Brooks?"

"Don't try and wriggle out of it," said the prefect.

Brooks slid to the ground and opened the bottom of the window wider.

"I'll do it tomorrow if Wall does it tonight. You want to go first, don't you, Wall?

Burnett was standing on top of his bed now, arms outstretched, his face streaked with tears, a weeping wraith in lemon-yellow pyjamas.

Thomas took his book from his side-table and found his place. It was still just light enough to read, although he knew it would strain his eyes. He heard the other boys dragging Burnett off his bed and over the linoleum; the squeak of the window frame; convulsive sobbing. If Matron came in now, this second, then Thomas would be in trouble for reading after lights out. But at least he would be the only one still in bed.

"Don't try to get back in, Burnett. We won't let you."

"Towards the *other* window, idiot. Can't you see they're waving to you?"

"Try not to look down!"

"Move!"

"That's more like it!"

Although he could hear the words of his book inside his head, they meant nothing to Thomas. He went back to the top of the page.

Brook's voice this time: "The mortar's worn just above that brick there. To your *right* … if you put your hand …"

A dry, powdery trickle seconds before the crack and crumble, the coming away of masonry. A long cry … the thud and crunch on the gravel.

Silence. Then a collective intake of breath: the most eloquent horror. Thomas knew that those closest to the window would be leaning out, studying the head, its perhaps unnatural angle to the body, the twist of the torso, the positions of arms and legs. He turned a page; replaced the leather marker before returning the book to the side table. He put his head on his pillow, his face turned away from the window.

"To your *left*," said Brooks, his tone neutral. "Yes, that was what I intended to say."

Another July, just before Thomas went on to his senior school. The drive to the house, a glimpse of the sea, waves apparently static for an instant: white ice of froth fixed on the motionless bay. Then the car angled into a dip; the estate wilder;

the great trees, their darker, luxuriant gloss; a herd of toffee-coloured cows in high lush grass; the hedge with a flitting of dunnocks. At last the ascent up a gentle hill and the house itself on the promontory. Terraced lawns and topiaries at the front; a dovecot in the shape of a keep. Had the cupola with a weather vane been there last time – right in centre of the roof, above the portico?

His father parked at a slight distance from the house. This time the sky seemed even further off, its blue roof high above the cirrus. A white sun spiked at its zenith. As he followed his father up the steps, he saw that again the front door was wide open. Yet this time there was no sea framed by the arch; instead, there was a garden, unlike that at the front of the house: the trees, more delicate – cross-hatched with soft leaves, the slender branches painted on silkscreen; unfamiliar flowers, their colours bright on the watery green of rare grasses; a giant snail crossing a tiny wooden bridge; branches of paths and rivers so similar as to appear almost interchangeable. The whole scene was imbued with faint quivering light that also suggested moisture seeping through. Thomas wondered for a moment whether the door opposite was closed. Was he looking at a *trompe l'oeil*, beyond which the true sea was hidden? As he was about to ask his father, the janitor appeared on the threshold. Instead of coming to meet them, he remained quite still, watching them, the parents on either side of their son, though they were no longer holding Thomas's hands.

As he followed the janitor into the hall, he understood that the house was only one room deep. In the garden, still visible through the door on the other side, a tiny green bird flew from a branch down to an ornamental bush. This movement created a sense of perspective too accurate to be an illusion.

"Your parents tell me you have no hobbies at school," said the janitor. "Is that correct?"

"I'm not sure. I went to Stamp Club once or twice."

The janitor walked towards a tall cabinet made from red-brown wood that had been burnished to a fluid gleam. His well-cut clothes, exquisitely trimmed beard and commanding air was unlike the casual appearance and manners of the caretaker at Thomas's school. Yet as the man glanced down at him, Thomas was conscious of an ambiguity he could not explain.

"Have a look at these," he said, beckoning Thomas to join him.

The janitor opened the double door to reveal a row of narrow wooden drawers, each one with a shiny brass handle. He was wearing white gloves. Slowly he slid out the top drawer and displayed a mahogany tray filled with coins. He picked one up and showed it to Thomas. On one side the smooth features of an Emperor; on the obverse face, a latticed gate, an entrance to a city or temple.

The next coin depicted a double-headed man; both profiles were bearded. The round spaces left behind in the tray exposed not wood but red felt discs.

"Who is it?" asked Thomas.

"Someone people once prayed to at important times. When they wanted to make a fresh start or move to another country. You're starting at a new school, aren't you?"

At that point Thomas realised that his parents were no longer beside him. "Where are my …"

"They called him *pater* too," said the janitor, carefully replacing the coin with the double-headed man in the tray.

Recollecting the encounter many years later, Thomas was unable to picture himself as he left the house and rejoined his parents outside. His thoughts on his way home remained with him, in one form or another, for many years. The replacement of the sea by a garden seemed impossible and at odds with what he knew of the estate and its surrounding geography. But there was a view of the sea before one reached the house. Had he misremembered his first visit, replacing the view of a garden seen through the door with an image of the sea? Why was it that the garden on the far side of the house bore no resemblance to the terraces and grounds at the front? Not to be found in any reference book, the small bird was neither a greenfinch nor a parakeet. Many years of casual research in the birding books he was fond of proved only that it was apparently unknown to ornithology.

On his way down, he'd counted the steps, finding solace in the clarity of numbers.

On his first day at senior school he met Thane Brooks, who was coming out of a Maths lesson. As Thomas loitered at the end of the queue waiting to enter, it was easy for Thane to draw him to one side without obstructing the flow into the classroom.

"How sad," said Thane, showing no surprise at their meeting, "that we're not in the same set. But never mind. I'll catch up with you soon."

Thomas hadn't seen Thane since the morning after Burnett's death. The Headmaster's inquisition lasted until well after midnight. Once it was established that no blame could be attached to him, Thomas stayed in bed, listening to the sound of appalled adult voices on the path, the words not quite audible. He heard the arrival of what he assumed was an ambulance. The members of his dormitory filed out one by one. Neither the prefect nor Brooks had returned by the time he fell asleep. When the wake-up bell rang at 7.00, there were three empty beds. The following morning, he found out the ambulance had been driven straight across the croquet lawn. At assembly it was announced there had been an accident. Burnett had been pronounced dead on his arrival at hospital. Two more boys would be leaving the school.

Thomas passed through the entrance hall during first break later that same morning. Nineteenth-century pictures of rural pursuits and a full-length oil painting of a previous proprietor in a gilt frame. Neatly arranged country magazines rested on a polished table. The whole was in contrast to the bare boards, cracked linoleum, cold corridors and classrooms with leaking radiators that lay beyond. Thane sat on a highly decorated wooden settle with red cushions. Hugh was next to him, his head leaning on his brother's shoulder, his long-lashed eyes shut, even though it was mid-morning. Both boys were still in school uniform, but their black leather suitcases were beside them. As Thane caught Thomas's eye, his smile was wistful but confident, the expression of one who knows his victory has merely been deferred. He did not say goodbye.

Although they were in the same year at senior school, Thomas had no immediate close contact with Thane. They'd been placed in different houses and sets; he only glimpsed his enemy in the distance: running across the quadrangle as the lunch bell was rung; kneeling down in his games kit to tie up a loose bootlace; collecting a prize at Assembly. Thomas learnt to be late for Maths; to approach the classroom from a direction opposite to wherever Thane Brooks was coming from. For hours he'd forget they were in the same school, an advantage of being in a larger institution.

Then a fortnight after the beginning of term, Thomas noticed in Chapel that Thane had inveigled himself into a pew directly opposite his. Everyone in the congregation was singing, except for Thane, who was staring intently at him. A smile played on his lips that did not shape for a single note. His expression, neither one of amusement nor happiness, suggested some greater knowledge, an absolute assurance that a greater force would act through him.

The junior house match took place on one of the pitches furthest from the main building. The mountains on the far side of the border were blue and charcoal grey; the damp green of the pine trees on the verge of turning black. A westerly wind carried spikes of rain tipped with hail horizontally across the pitch. The heavens swirled with damaged light and rainclouds, dark tufts detached from higher cumuli nimbus; white shafts glittered for a second before being reconfigured in the wild travelling sky. Even new boys understood that matches were never cancelled, however inimical the weather.

Thomas's tracksuit became sodden and heavy even before he reached the pitch. Within a minute of the whistle, his hair was plastered flat against his skull, his shirt stuck to his back, boots mired in mud. He wasn't aware of Brooks until tackled crisply from the side; the ball shooting into touch at the very instant he felt an elbow rap his ribs. A minute later, trying to head the ball, he was sent spinning to the ground. As Thomas picked himself up, Brooks gave him a little wave. Then it was the full repertoire of his enemy's tricks: tugs and palm-offs on the blind side; the studs somehow dislodging a shin pad and riding across bare flesh; the tackle never so high as to be easily observable, instead the subtlest of trips; the stamp on the toecap concealed by a clever feint. The referee, his glasses speckled and smudged by rain, wobbled yards behind the ball, his whistle rarely raised to his mouth. Thomas strayed far out on the wing, distancing himself from play, making no attempt to keep level with the attack. He was shivering, his blue hands tucked into his trousers. Then he saw Thane, pouncing from the spray to drive the ball fiercely, full into Thomas's face. A feeble phrase of admonition from the referee. Then Thane bending over him, offering his victim a hand. Thomas felt the blood flowing from his nose, salty on his cracked lips. As they were standing together, and before the referee squelched his way over, Thane curled his arm round Thomas in apparent commiseration. He hissed into his ear: "How many times is a wall worth rebuilding, Wall?"

II

Still in the prison of his pin-stripes, Thomas sat in an armchair watching his father dying on the sofa. The sitting-room offered a view of a dishevelled December garden: a beech blocking half of the light: a parti-coloured lawn of moss and clumps of grass; hedges and shrubs with heavy foliage, untrimmed since May.

"And so how was it?" asked his father.

"They want me to work till midnight," he explained.

Since his father's premature retirement, they'd moved to a smaller house; the mortgage was still unpaid. To avoid debt, Thomas declined a place at university to work in the City. His mother had died during his final year of sixth-form college and now it seemed certain his father would follow her within months. Although an only child, he'd no expectation of a considerable inheritance. Much of his parents' money had been spent on the misery that was his supposedly prestigious education at private schools, none of which were well known outside their own localities.

"But is it interesting?"

"Perhaps it will become so."

The disease had refined his father's features, revealing the precise angle of the bones. He resembled an ascetic, forgotten and left to fast in a wilderness. How could he tell his father he'd hated his job from the first? He must preserve the illusion he was settled in the City and had good prospects.

"Father, do you remember the house you took me to when I was much younger? The place looked after by a janitor, as the man who owned it was never at home."

"I can't say I do. Where was it?"

"A house by the sea. I'm not sure which county it was in. It was quite a large building set in its own grounds. I think it was part of an estate."

Ever since starting work, Thomas had found himself thinking of the house and its inhabitant: the terraced gardens at the front, its situation on a cliff overlooking the sea; a copper coin held in the palm of a white gloved hand.

"I'm sorry … I've no recollection of it. Are you sure it wasn't somewhere you went with your mother?"

"You were both there. Although on the last occasion you stayed outside when I went into the house."

A tremor of pain ran through his father. His face turned the pallor of dead flesh; his white hand gripped the red rug. *It's just a question of trying to keep him as comfortable as possible*, the doctor had announced that morning.

"I'm sorry," said his father. Even his irises seemed to be losing colour, the pupils dark against

44

a paler background. "I've no idea what you're talking about. I think my memory still works. But perhaps it isn't what it was."

"The janitor showed me a collection of coins – although you weren't with us at the time."

"Coin … coins?" his father repeated the word as if it were in a foreign language.

Outside, the garden edged closer to invisibility; the hedges no longer had more than a hint of green; the leaves and delicate branch-work now almost metallic, as though they had been wrought by hand.

"I'll go and change, if you don't mind." Thomas felt like an impostor in his pin-stripes.

"What?"

"My suit. I'm going to take it off."

In his room, staring out at the suburban street, its small front gardens and hedges slowly turning to black bars patched with lamplight, he wondered at the inescapable strangeness of the ordinary. Even though he'd been living in this house and road for more than two months, his life in such surroundings seemed no more than a conjuring trick: all less real than the house by the sea and the coin in the janitor's hand. Yet hadn't he understood that even in that place, where every step up to the door could be counted, there was something not yet fully experienced? The views through the entrance – both permeated with the mystery of undecided destinations.

❖

In his second job in the City, Thomas Wall met a man who'd been in the same house as Thane Brooks. Nathaniel de Brachy worked for a pensions firm that wished to diversify its portfolio. As Thomas had left his senior school at the first half term of his opening academic year, he wouldn't have recognised him but for his distinctive name. They'd both been in Coin Club.

"You won't remember me," Thomas added, after introducing himself. "We were new boys, but I only completed the first seven weeks."

"Coin Club! That takes me back. Didn't they have a grand name for it?

"Yes, the master in charge called it the Numismatics Society."

"That's right. I suppose I must have sensed even then that I'd end up working in something to do with money."

Nathaniel was tall with the features of an enervated Plantagenet prince.

"You were in the same house as Thane Brooks."

"Now there's someone I'd be happy to forget. You've a good memory for someone who lasted such a short time."

"It was because of Brooks that I left. We were at prep school together. Fortunately he was expelled."

46

A mid-morning sun instilled the office with a hard bright light; every object – the desk, the lap top, the steel and glass coffee table, was unequivocally itself. Despite this, the mention of Thane had added depth to a shadow in the far corner.

"Yes," replied de Brachy, gazing out of the window; the empires of finance basking in high-rises, glittering and impervious. "He was quite a piece of work, wasn't he? He didn't stay the course, but during his time with us, two boys in the house died and one was seriously injured. Nothing was ever proved, but we all had a feeling Brooks was behind it. The head man found an excuse to move him on. After that, everything was fine."

"Did you ever feel …"

"For some reason," said de Brachy with a distant smile, "he left me alone. I've no idea why."

Then they discussed investment trusts, trackers and fund managers.

In the months that followed Thomas tried to dismiss the notion he'd been selected by Thane Brooks: that another meeting was inevitable. He tracked down newspaper reports of the tragedies at his senior school, but they were brief and gave little away. Then he married, moved to an even better job in the Square Mile and failed to think about Brooks for months at a time. In his office, he was the only person with children who didn't send them to boarding school. When asked, he never gave the real reason.

The first intimations of Thane's return came in late middle-age. A beach holiday abroad. Trying to reach an island just off shore, Thomas swam too far out to sea. The waves that had looked so innocuous from a table on the hotel terrace became choppier; a crosscurrent was dragging him away from his destination. He'd been under twice and was spitting water when a man in a launch rescued him.

That evening, Brooks was seated at the bar reading the local newspaper. Then Thomas realised his mistake, and that whoever it was, he was in his early twenties. He left at once and went into the town. By the time he returned there was no sign of the man. He never came across him in the hotel again. On the day he was flying home, he saw Thane's name in the register, right below his own.

Shortly before his first heart attack, Thomas attended an investment conference in the north of England. At lunch, there was a loud group at a table near his, baying across their empty bottles of Beaune and Bordeaux. A bearded man in dark suit, less bibulous than the others, caught his eye and smiled in a manner both familiar and unsettling. Thomas was close enough to see there was no name tag on the man's lapel.

Thomas turned to his colleague. "Do you know the bloke sitting over there? Beard ... pale face."

"I had a word with him over coffee this morning."

"What's his name?"

"I can't recall. But I can tell you what he does."

"Oh?"

"He's an arms dealer. He seemed cordial enough, even when I explained I was running an ethical investment trust. No tobacco; no guns or anything of that sort. He has a brother in pharmaceuticals. Trying to develop a new type of sleeping pill."

Early that afternoon, after coming out of the washroom in the basement, Thomas went the wrong way down a passage. He passed empty subterranean seminar rooms and disused hospitality suites. As he wheeled round, he saw a boy of about fourteen padding towards him. What was a child doing at an event aimed at stockbrokers, company directors and investment bankers? The strip lighting was subdued, emitting only a hazy yellow illumination and an electrical hum. When they were about to pass each other, the boy stared up at him: Thane Brooks, which was patently impossible. Thomas hurried on down the corridor. Fortunately, his presentation was on soon. Then, with apologies but no explanation to his colleague, he caught the first train to Liverpool Street. On the way down, unable to read or do anything except find the buffet bar, he tried to reproach himself for having panicked: the poor light; he'd only seen the boy for a moment; he and Thane Brooks were about the same age – he put the whole incident down to his imagination. He'd imposed Brooks's features on a boy who was probably the son of a cleaner or kitchen worker. No doubt it had happened because the man with a beard had born a faint resemblance to Brooks as Thomas thought he might look now.

The late *Evening Standard* reported the death of a prominent businessman who'd been attending a conference in the north.

Early retirement through ill health gave Thomas time to reflect on formative things: the death of Burnett in the dormitory; his failure to complete a single term at his first senior school; his decision to forgo university. He'd been driving all afternoon and was now lost somewhere in the west of England. It would be best to stop at a road house and borrow a map, but he could make out nothing except ploughed fields beneath a pale sun quarried from a granite January sky, a farmstead in the middle distance and a tract of moorland beyond.

When he missed a turning, he'd been thinking about Thane Brooks; the evening his enemy first put in an appearance at the Numismatics Society. His initial choice of activity, he told the master in charge, had proved unsatisfactory. Thane's calling card was a Roman coin, an emperor on one side. As the boys gathered round, Thomas stood at the back, craning forward just far enough to mimic an interest. Most of the boys left when the bell for the end of activities rang. Thomas lingered behind, engaging the master in awkward conversation. When he went out, Thane was waiting for him in the corridor.

"I don't think you saw the other side, did you?" Thane whispered, falling in beside him.

"Well, never mind. You'll find out soon enough."

It was difficult to complain about such a seemingly anodyne observation; impossible to convey the menace behind the innocent tone. The next week he feigned illness to avoid his evening activity.

On the way back to school from half term, Thomas was sitting on the back seat of the Rover, a paper bag of uneaten boiled sweets in his lap, *Sing Something Simple* on the Radio, when he wept with a passion that seemed to his parents to presage a breakdown. He couldn't go back; yet would not explain the reason. His father stopped in a lay-by, but Thomas was immune to mere words, possibly at the edge of hysteria. His father reversed. The car headed back in the direction of home. There followed a period of recovery; the tedium of tutors; an absence of friends. A year later he was pronounced fit to attend the local grammar school. Never once did he regret the end of his boarding school education.

At nightfall, he pulled off the main road. It was miles before he came to cottages grouped around a green, some semblance of a village, a low inn frowning beneath its thatch but at least offering accommodation. He registered and was in bed before he remembered that he'd forgotten to ask where he was.

The next morning, he awoke early. Although places were laid in the breakfast room, there was no movement in the kitchen. In the bar, the towels were over the beer pumps. He listened: no creak on the floorboards above him; not a sound of water stirring in the pipes or the low hums and clicks of the central heating system. Outside, a fine blue day, a hint of snow on the far hills. He'd settled up the previous night. Why not go now?

Seated in the car, he could no longer recall the direction he'd come from, but the road that curved alluringly to his right was well maintained. *This will lead me somewhere*, he thought, driving off in that direction.

At first, the countryside was unremarkable; high hedges prohibited a view of the landscape. Odd that there were no signposts. Yet he'd been unable to suppress the notion that he was heading towards the coast. The road dipped sharply. Hedges gave way to stone walls and a vista of open fields, the furrows mailed with frost, and for a moment spots of white sunlight catching a blade of sea. Now he was in a sheltered valley. The evergreens crisp with vestigial snow, cows wading in a pool of mist, a hazy stream: there was something familiar yet half hidden, about this place; as if he were moving, not in the present, but through a memory, imperfectly recovered. Then he understood that he'd chanced upon the estate. Once more he was heading up a gentle slope: there were the terraces, the great trees and the topiaries; the house with its steps and cupola.

He parked and got out of the car. The air was colder; feeling a sharp twist of pain in his hardened arteries, he put his hand to his heart. About him, everything gleamed, as if motionless and trapped under glass, preserved in the grip of an eternal January. Was his blood still circulating through his damaged veins? He forced himself up the first step leading to the house. The doors were shut. Perhaps he should return. But when he glanced back he saw his car had gone. For a second, he held a vision of it, bonnet down in a ditch, back wheels spinning. Then Thane Brooks was walking silently towards him, not one dark pace disturbing the air. Neither a child nor an adult, he appeared as fully himself at last: a pale youth, purveyor of the dark drive, the gift of conclusions.

"Don't worry," he said. "The janitor is in and anyway I have the key." As he drew level with Thomas, his smile was no longer terrifying but a token of a great peace. "My final touch is always gentle."

As Thomas turned towards the doors, he understood they were about to open. But what would be revealed: the owner in his garden or the sea?

www.ingramcontent.com/pod-product-compliance
Lightning Source LLC
Chambersburg PA
CBHW031419200726
48285CB00017BA/2567